FREEZE

FReeZe

CHRIS PRIESTLEY

Barrington Stoke

For Alex

First published in 2021 in Great Britain by
Barrington Stoke Ltd
18 Walker Street, Edinburgh, EH3 7LP

www.barringtonstoke.co.uk

Text & Illustrations © 2021 Chris Priestley

A CIP catalogue record for this book is available from the British Library upon request

ISBN: 978-1-78112-983-8

Printed by Hussar Books, Poland

CONTENTS

CHAPTER 1

Maya woke with a jolt when the music started playing, not sure for a moment where she was. She gave her radio alarm clock a smack to stop the music, knocking it off the bedside table and sending it clattering to the floor.

Maya jumped up to check if the alarm clock was broken. Her mum had bought it for her to make sure she always woke up for school. She was relieved to see it still seemed to be working.

Maya opened the curtains, squinting into the cloudy daylight. She looked out over the estate, across the canal, past the old factory and the common towards the school. She suddenly had an intense feeling that something bad was going to happen.

She just didn't know what …

Maya felt like she was walking in cobwebs as she went into the kitchen. There was something hiding in the darkness at the back of her mind.

A dream. It had been a bad dream. But she could not remember what shape the dream had taken.

Her phone pinged. It was Maya's mother texting her from work to make sure she was awake and ready for school, just like she did every morning.

Maya normally did not mind – she knew her mother had to work. They needed the money.

But that morning she wished her mother was there. Just for a brief hug.

Maya got dressed, ate her breakfast and headed out of the flat to walk to school. When she got there, she found her friends Carla, Jason and Tomas outside the library.

Mrs Vargas, the librarian, was making sure everyone went in calmly. Maya joined her friends as they filed inside and then they all slumped down at the table in the far corner.

"What's the matter with you?" said Carla to Maya. "You look terrible."

"Cheers," said Maya.

"Sorry," said Carla. "But you do look a bit shattered."

"I had a really bad night," said Maya. "I had this horrible nightmare. Really bad. I haven't had a dream as bad as that since I was little."

"What?" said Carla. "That's weird. Me too. What was yours about?"

"I don't know," said Maya. "I forgot it straight away. I just remember how terrified I was. I keep thinking I'm going to remember, but it's like the nightmare is so scary my brain won't let me think of it. How about you? What was yours about?"

"I can't remember either," said Carla. "Maybe we had the same one."

"Yeah," said Maya, rolling her eyes. "Maybe."

"That stuff really happens, you know," said Carla.

Maya didn't say anything. She was too tired to have some stupid conversation about dreams. Carla always had all these weird ideas about supernatural stuff.

Jason turned round from chatting to Tomas. "Wait, are you two talking about nightmares?" Jason asked. "This is so strange. Me and Tomas were just saying how we both had nightmares too. Last night. Really bad ones, but we can't—"

"You can't remember," said Carla. She looked at Maya. "See?!"

Maya shook her head.

"But that's pretty weird, huh?" said Jason.

"Don't get Carla started," said Maya. "You know what she's—"

"OK, OK," said Mrs Varga, cutting Maya off. "Please all settle down. As you know, Miss Miller is away today and we have a supply teacher visiting us. Let's try to show that we are not a total rabble. I'm looking at you, Maya."

"Why me, Miss?" said Maya.

Carla laughed but stopped suddenly as a man stepped forward from behind one of the bookshelves.

"Hello, everyone," he said. "My name is Mr Kumar. I'm taking this lesson today. Hopefully it'll be fun."

Mr Kumar went to the white board and wrote "CREEPY STORY" in big letters.

"Today we're going to be writing a creepy story," he said. "So I hope you've all got your creepy heads on."

"Carla's always got her creepy head on, sir," said Maya.

Jason laughed loudly.

"Maya, come here," said Mrs Varga, waving at Maya to come to her.

"What, Miss?" said Maya.

"I don't want you and Carla sitting together," Mrs Varga explained.

"But—" Maya started to say.

"Over here," said Mrs Varga. "Come on." She pointed to an empty table.

"On my own?" said Maya.

Carla laughed.

Maya slumped into a chair, scowling.

Mrs Varga went behind her desk and took the register. Maya felt like it was going to be a long day.

Maya leaned back in her chair and saw someone she didn't recognise standing outside the library door. It was a girl in a silver coat with a fur-lined hood.

The door opened slowly and the girl came in. She walked straight towards Maya's table and took off her silver coat. The girl put the coat on the back of the chair and sat down opposite Maya.

"Er – who are you?" said Maya.

"New," the girl said with a smile.

This new girl was the palest person Maya had ever seen. Her skin was so white, while her hair was jet black.

"OK," said Mr Kumar. "Let's crack on. Everyone should have a piece of paper and something to write with."

Maya took a pen out of her bag and grabbed a sheet of the lined paper Mrs Varga had left on the table. She started to doodle in the top-left corner.

"So I want you to come up with some really creepy story ideas," said Mr Kumar. "When I say 'creepy', I mean properly creepy – not gory."

There was a groan from one of the boys behind Maya and she smiled. What was it with boys and gore?

"We've all got things that creep us out, haven't we?" Mr Kumar went on. "Think about that. Think about what creeps you out."

"Puppets," said Maya.

"Don't just shout out, Maya," said Mrs Varga.

"Oh yes," said Mr Kumar. "Puppets and dolls. Very creepy. OK, what if the creepy story is set in the wintertime? What comes into your mind when I say winter?"

"Snow?" said Tomas.

"Good," said Mr Kumar. "Anything else?"

"Snowmen," said Tomas.

Carla laughed.

"What?" said Tomas.

"You might not think of snowmen as creepy, but maybe we could make them so," said Mr Kumar.

"Yes, I think we could," said Tomas, frowning at Carla.

"OK," said Mr Kumar. "Anything else?"

Now hands went up all round the room.

Mr Kumar wrote every suggestion up on the white board.

"Ice," said someone.

"Icicles."

"Frost."

"Snowballs."

Carla laughed again.

"Shhh," said Mrs Varga.

"Christmas."

"Christmas. Yes. We could have a whole other board full of things just about Christmas, couldn't we? Maybe we'll do that nearer to Christmas if I come back."

Maya sighed at the idea of doing even more writing. She could not wait for the Christmas holidays.

"We won't waste a lot of time trying to agree on a location," said Mr Kumar. "Instead, I thought we'd set the stories here, in this town, even in this school if you want to. And set your stories in the present so you don't have to worry about any historical details or old-fashioned language. Imagine your story has four characters: two boys and two girls. Just call them the four friends. You don't have to worry about names. You can always give them names later on. Have a think about what your story could be for a few minutes. Put your name at the top."

Maya stared at the board with the list of wintery words and then at her sheet of paper. She did not have one single idea. Her mind was as blank as the paper.

The new girl started writing straight away. Maya took a sneaky look at what she had written at the top of the page: "Winter".

"Ha!" said Maya. "That's where your name is supposed to go, not the title."

"That *is* my name," the new girl said.

"What?" said Maya. "Your name's Winter?"

The new girl smiled and nodded.

"Weird," said Maya.

Winter shrugged.

Maya suddenly realised Mr Kumar had moved and was standing right beside her.

"Any thoughts about a story yet?" he asked.

Maya tapped her pen on the table. Why was he not asking the new girl? She looked like she had a ton of ideas.

Maya shook her head. Mr Kumar smiled.

Everyone around her had their heads down, writing. As always, Maya felt like she was the only one struggling. Even Carla was writing away. Jason had his tongue sticking out as he focused.

"OK," Mr Kumar said after twenty minutes. "Would anyone like to read the start of their story? I know it's hard to be first, but it would be great if someone was brave."

To Maya's surprise, Tomas put his hand up.

Mr Kumar smiled and nodded.

Tomas took a deep breath.

"My story is called 'Snow', sir," said Tomas.

Maya was surprised at how confident Tomas sounded as he started to tell his story. Tomas didn't say much in class normally and she liked that about him. It was like if Tomas didn't need to say anything, he didn't. She was jealous of that. Maya always felt like she had to say something, and she wished she didn't.

As Tomas read, Maya began to picture herself as part of his story. The four friends were not just nameless students – they were Maya, Carla, Jason and Tomas. Maya could see

the story as clearly as anything. It felt real.
Completely real. She was right there.

CHAPTER 2

The four friends were walking down a corridor one day when they saw a crowd of students gathered together, laughing and pointing.

"What's going on?" said Maya as the friends joined the back of the crowd.

"No idea," said Carla. "It's got everyone all excited whatever it is."

They shoved their way forward and everyone went quiet, apart from a girl right at the front in a silver hooded coat. She was muttering something under her breath. Maya pushed her aside to get a better look.

There was a nervous giggle from the back of the group.

Now Maya and the others could see a large painting of snowmen. Four snowmen. The snowmen each had branches for arms and twigs for hands. They were standing in the street at night, lit by a street light.

The snowmen's faces were really strange. They were not the jolly, friendly looking snowmen you saw on Christmas cards. These looked like they had melted and all their features had drooped and then refrozen.

But that was not all. Under each snowman was a name: Carla, Jason, Maya and Tomas.

Laughter rippled in the crowd as students began to head off.

"Look at them," said Carla, pointing to the snowmen. "They're so ugly. And who does a painting of snowmen standing around in the dark? It's weird."

The bell rang and the four friends went off to their lessons. But they kept walking past the painting all day.

"Don't you think there's something creepy about that painting?" said Maya as they went past it yet again.

"You're imagining things," said Carla.

"At least it's almost home time," said Maya. "Thank goodness."

"Er ... have you forgotten?" said Tomas. "We're in detention."

Maya groaned. "All because you were giggling in Assembly, Carla."

"What?" said Carla. "It was you!"

"Who cares?" said Jason. "All I know is it wasn't me and I'm still getting detention."

"Wait," said Maya. "They've moved."

"Who's moved?" said Tomas.

"The snowmen," said Maya. "In the painting."

Carla laughed.

"Moved how?" said Jason.

"They've swapped places," said Maya.

"They can't have!" said Jason.

"No," said Tomas. "Maya's right. The one called Carla was on the left before. Now it's on the right."

"What?" said Carla. "What are you on about? Paintings don't move. It must be another painting."

"Why would anyone do the same painting but with the snowmen in different places?" said Jason.

"I don't know," said Carla. "People are weird."

"Well, whoever it is, they're laughing at us and I'm not having it," said Maya.

She climbed up on a chair and grabbed one edge of the painting.

"Don't, Maya," said Tomas. "If you tear it up, everyone will know it's us."

"What do you care?" said Maya. "Do you know who did it?"

"No," said Tomas. "Of course I don't."

"Tomas is right," said Carla. "People will know it's us."

"So?" Maya said. "Don't worry. I'm just going to take the painting down and hide it somewhere. I'm not going to damage it."

But just as Maya said that, she slipped from the chair and the painting ripped in half in her hands.

"Maya!" said Tomas.

"What?" said Maya. "It was an accident."

"What's going on?" said a voice behind them. It was Miss Miller coming down the corridor as the bell went for the end of the day.

Maya rushed to stuff the two halves of the painting behind a cupboard before Miss Miller arrived.

"Off to the study room for your detention," said Miss Miller. With a sigh, Maya and the others followed her.

*

The four friends came out of detention an hour later and headed along the corridor to go home.

"What ...?" said Maya, looking at the wall. "How ...?"

They all just stared at each other, amazed. The painting of the snowmen was back up on the wall. Not only that – it was back in one piece. But it had not been repaired. There was no sign it had ever been ripped at all.

"That's not possible," said Jason.

"I know," said Carla. "But look at it."

"I'm getting away from that thing," said Maya. "Come on."

They left the school and found it had snowed. And it hadn't just snowed a bit. It was the heaviest snowfall any of them had ever seen – a super-thick blanket of snow over everything.

"Wow!" said Jason. He skidded to a halt as the snow kept on falling around them.

The four friends all stood staring at the scene in front of them. It was so beautiful. Even the school car park and gates looked pretty in the snow.

But it also seemed a bit spooky to Maya. Everything was so quiet. There were no sounds at all. The snow must have stopped the traffic, because normally there was some noise – cars or buses or taxis or something. But the only sound was their own breathing.

"Come on!" Jason rushed forward. The others followed him out of the school gates, whooping and stopping to make snowballs.

The snow was the perfect consistency for snowballs and made a wonderful soft crunching noise under their feet. Maya was already wishing she had thicker socks on. Her feet were freezing.

The streets around the school were deserted. It felt like they were the only people around for miles.

"Where is everyone?" said Jason. "It's only five o'clock and it's like the middle of the night."

Something moved up ahead in the darkness. Someone in a silver hooded coat.

"Hey!" shouted Tomas.

But whoever it was vanished. They seemed to be alone again.

"Wait," said Maya. "What are those?"

"What?" said Carla.

"Over there!" Maya pointed down the street.

There were four snowmen. Just like the ones in the painting. And just like in the

painting, the snowmen were lit up by the harsh light of an overhead street light.

"Let's get out of here!" said Maya, and led the others up a side street. But she soon came to a halt again.

"Look!" said Maya. "There."

There were four more strange snowmen standing under a street light at the end of the road they'd turned into.

"How many snowmen are there round here?" said Jason.

"I don't know," said Carla. "But it's freaking me out."

The four friends all looked at each other, their scared faces showing it wasn't just Carla that was freaked out.

When they looked back to the snowmen, they had gone.

"Wait!" said Jason. "That's not possible. Th ... That's not right. It can't be!"

"They can't just have vanished," said Tomas. "Stuff doesn't just appear and disappear. That's rubbish!"

"The snowmen haven't disappeared," Maya said softly. "Look. They've moved."

The friends all followed Maya's gaze and gasped. The four strange snowmen were across the road from them now.

"Snowmen don't move," said Jason.

The street light above the snowmen flickered and went out, making Maya squeal. The light came back on right away. But the snowmen were gone again.

"Run!" shouted Jason, and he started sprinting off, with the others close behind.

It was difficult to run in the snow and Maya was not a great runner anyway. She went as fast as her legs would take her through the thick snow, but it was hard work. It wasn't long before Maya stopped, exhausted and gasping for breath. The air was so cold it hurt to breathe.

Her friends had come to a halt ahead of her under another street light. Maya managed to catch up after a moment. They were trying to catch their breath and make sense of what was happening when this light flickered and went out too.

The four friends all screamed this time. The darkness seemed almost solid – like a thick blanket had been thrown over them. Maya felt like her heart was about to explode … and then the light suddenly came back on.

"Phew," said Jason, but he wasn't relieved for long.

The snowmen were back. They were right up against the friends, pinning them against the wall. Maya could feel the chill coming from them.

The snowmen seemed bigger now, their faces twisted into frozen scowls. Their crooked twig hands began to twitch and reach out towards the friends, grabbing at their clothes and faces.

The snowman nearest to Maya grasped at her, its twig hands closing round her arm. Maya opened her mouth to scream, but the snowman's other "hand" grabbed her face and muffled the sound. Then the street light went out and they were plunged into pitch-darkness again.

*

Maya eventually managed to cry out but realised she was in the library, not outside in the street. Tomas had finished his story and everyone was looking at her.

"That was really great," said Mr Kumar. "Well done, Tomas. Very creepy indeed. It certainly worked on Maya."

Carla laughed. Maya looked down at her hands, feeling embarrassed.

"How about anyone else?" said Mr Kumar.

To Maya's surprise, Carla put her hand up. It wasn't that Carla wasn't a good writer. Maya had read some of her stuff. She was good. And Carla wasn't shy about it. Maya was surprised because Carla hardly ever put her hand up.

Carla was more of a heckler. She rolled her eyes when people answered questions in class. She laughed when they got something wrong or tripped over their words. Carla was Maya's best friend, but it was hard to like that side of her.

"Hello," Mr Kumar said. "What's your name?"

"Carla."

"What have you come up with, Carla?" said Mr Kumar.

"I was remembering how my dad told me that people used to have races on the canal when it froze over," Carla said. "You know, the canal down the road by the old factory?"

"Really?" said Mr Kumar. "I never knew that."

"It all stopped after there was a terrible accident one year," Carla explained. "The ice gave way and lots of children fell into the water and drowned."

"Horrible," said Mr Kumar. "I didn't know that either. Let's hear your story then."

"It's called 'Ice'," said Carla.

Carla started to read her story and once again Maya imagined it so clearly. Like it was a memory of something Maya had experienced rather than something Carla was making up.

CHAPTER 3

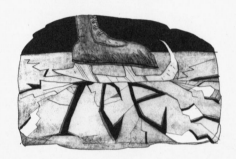

One day, the four friends walked along the canal that ran past the old factory. It was so cold that winter that the canal had frozen over for the first time in years.

"Whoah!" said Jason, looking at the ice down below. "That's amazing."

It did look amazing, Maya had to agree. The canal was normally a grim and gloomy place, but the freezing weather had transformed it. The still, dark water had been replaced by a twinkling sheet of ice.

There were stories on the news about how in Victorian times people would skate down the canal when it was frozen. Kids from the factory had skating races and hundreds of people lined the canals to watch and cheer.

The factory had closed down long ago. Plans had been put forward to renovate it and turn it into offices and flats and an arts centre, but it was still shut up. Most of the building was in a bad way. Kids broke into it sometimes. The windows had metal grilles over them and the walls were covered with graffiti.

The whole length of the canal beside the factory was frozen. It looked like the ice was completely solid, but the police had warned people not to go on it in case any of the ice was thin and cracked.

The police reminded everyone of the terrible tragedy that had happened during a Victorian skating race, when the ice had broken and

children had fallen into the freezing water and died.

Maya shivered. This place was really grim. They had done a project on Victorian factories and mills when they were in Year 6. She knew that children had worked in this place back then. Younger than Maya. Younger than any of them.

Maya tried to imagine what it must have been like to work there. How would she have coped with a life like that? Maya wondered if those children didn't mind because they had never known any different. Maya sometimes felt that living in this town was like being trapped in a very small box with very high walls, but it was nothing compared to the life those children had back then.

Maya saw some steps leading to the frozen surface of the canal and edged down them carefully. She held on to the rusty metal railing to stop herself from slipping.

"Maya!" shouted Carla. "Where are you going?"

"I just want to see what it's like to walk on," Maya said, stepping out onto the ice.

"I think you should get off the ice, Maya," said Jason, coming down the steps with Tomas and Carla. "The police said it isn't safe."

Maya sighed and rolled her eyes. Then she headed off across the ice.

"Stop!" shouted Carla. "Maya!"

"It's fine," said Maya, looking back and smiling. "It's rock solid. Don't be such chickens."

Carla, Tomas and Jason looked at each other.

"I dare you to walk with me to the canal lock gates," said Maya.

"No way," said Jason.

"Chicken!" said Maya again.

Maya knew Jason hated to be called that. Sure enough, he muttered to himself and stepped out onto the ice to stand beside her. Moments later, Tomas and Carla followed.

"Come on!" said Maya.

She set off towards the lock gates, but they suddenly seemed much further away and it was hard to walk on the ice. She kept slipping. So did the others.

"Stop, Maya!" shouted Carla. "Don't go too far ahead."

They went past the houseboats that were frozen in the ice, smoke rising up from their chimneys.

Then Maya noticed the girl in a silver hooded coat. She was standing watching them, looking down from the road. The sky was so black now that her silver coat glowed against the darkness.

Maya was going to point her out to the others, but when she looked back, the girl had gone.

Then Maya heard noises coming from inside the factory. Muffled sounds. Whispers. Giggling. The pattering of small feet on the stone floors. For some reason it made Maya feel even more unsteady and she almost fell on the ice.

The friends could see movement now, behind the metal grilles covering the windows.

"It's kids," said Jason. "There are kids in there."

"How did they get in?" said Carla. "The place is locked up."

Jason shrugged.

"There's always a way to break into places, isn't there?" said Tomas.

"You sound like an expert," said Carla.

Tomas blushed. "I'm just saying," he said.

"What are they doing anyway?" said Maya.

They could see the shapes of the children behind the grilles. They just seemed to be looking out, watching the four friends. Sometimes they would whisper to each other. Then there was a scratching sound. Like the children were raking their fingernails down the inside of the metal grilles.

"Oi!" shouted Carla. "What are you looking at?"

But the watching children didn't reply. They just giggled and ran away.

"You're not scaring anyone!" shouted Maya, although she was a bit scared. Those whispering shadows somehow made her feel even more wobbly on the ice. Her shout seemed to skid across the frozen canal and bounce back from the factory walls.

There were long icicles hanging from the edge of the factory roof. As Maya pointed to them, one fell off and smashed only a metre from where they were standing, making them all jump.

Then the four friends could hear shoes clattering and echoing inside the building as the children ran about. It sounded like there were hundreds of them in there.

"What's going on?" said Jason. "I think we should get out of here."

"It's just kids," said Maya. But she did not feel as confident as she tried to sound.

The noise of the footsteps died away for a moment, but then it seemed to come back in a different place. The footsteps were heading for the side of the factory that ran alongside an offshoot of the canal – near the lock gates ahead of them. The children's activity seemed to shake the building, and more icicles began snap off the roof.

"I think Jason's right," said Tomas. "We should go."

Before anyone could say anything else, there was a different sound. A strange noise, getting louder and louder, growing into a thunderous scraping and screeching.

"What is that noise?" shouted Maya. She clamped her hands over her ears as her friends did the same.

Then they noticed that the ice was shaking. It was like an earthquake. The ice was cracking

44

too. Maya grabbed Jason to stop herself from falling over.

"What's happening?" yelled Carla.

"I told you we should get off the ice," said Jason. "Come on."

But before the four friends could go anywhere, hundreds and hundreds of children came out from the offshoot of the canal, on the other side of the factory. They were pale and blurred, like they were behind thick, milky glass. Or ice. The more Maya tried to focus on the children's features, the less clear they were. They were moving so fast – like a shoal of fish.

She could see they were mostly boys and girls her own age, dressed in old-fashioned grey and brown clothes. The boys wore caps and the girls had shawls wrapped round them. They were all wearing skates.

They rushed towards Maya and her friends and passed straight through them with a whooshing sound before they could cry out. The children flowed through the four friends like a freezing cold wind, then came back again. Maya could hear them whispering to each other as they went, the sound mingling with the scraping of their skates on the ice.

Then all was quiet again. Maya and the others turned with wide eyes to see what was happening.

The skaters had come to a halt, making a huge crowd that filled the whole canal. Their eyes were hollow, their faces pale and sad. They reached out thin hands towards Maya and her friends.

Carla screamed and Maya grabbed hold of Tomas.

"W-what's going on?" said Jason. "Who are they? W-w-what are they?"

The skaters edged forward very slowly now, their skates cutting into the ice. The sound was like fingernails scratching on glass – a horrible, high-pitched screech.

"Run for the steps!" Maya called to the others.

She grabbed Carla by the arm and dragged her. Jason and Tomas followed, but the skaters were moving faster and began to catch up with them. The ice was being cut with their skates and started to crack all over its surface.

Maya slipped and fell. Jason helped her to her feet and she turned, seeing how close the ghostly children were now. One of them stared at Maya with big lifeless eyes and reached out his thin hand. It went straight into Maya's body. She felt the chill of the hand as it passed through her.

Maya saw the girl in the silver coat again. She was about to call for help when the ice collapsed, snapping, shattering. All four friends dropped into the freezing black waters below. Maya grabbed at the slippery fragments of ice in a desperate effort not to sink into the blackness. But soon she could see nothing, feel nothing ...

*

Maya gasped as she came back to the reality of the library. She almost felt like she had just emerged from the canal's freezing cold water.

Maya heard someone say, "Are you all right?" But she wasn't sure if she was still in the story or the dream or whatever it had been. Then she saw the new girl looking at her.

"What?" said Maya.

"I just wondered if you were all right," Winter said. "You looked distressed."

Distressed? thought Maya. *Who says "distressed"?*

"Well, I for one really enjoyed Carla's story," said Mr Kumar.

Carla was looking very pleased with herself.

"Now that Carla and Tomas have started us off with their stories, does anyone else feel up to sharing theirs?" Mr Kumar asked.

Jason put his hand up. Maya was still trying to shake off the effect of Carla's story. Maybe she could forget the freezing water by focusing on Jason's story.

"What's your wintery idea?" Mr Kumar asked Jason.

"A flood, sir," he said.

There was a small ripple of giggles, but Mr Kumar put his hand up.

"No, that's great," said Mr Kumar. "It's just as likely to flood in winter as it is to snow now. Actually much more likely, depending where you live. Flooding is a great idea. But how does it make a creepy story?"

"Well, sir, it's about the common," Jason said. "My dad told me that there's a burial pit there. From when this town was just a village. He said that one year there was a terrible winter that went on for ages and loads of people died."

"And how does your story start?" asked Mr Kumar.

"Well, I thought the four friends go to the common and see the flood rising up at night."

"OK," said Mr Kumar. "That's a nice image – I like it. What's next?"

Maya saw the floodwater like a flashback in a movie. She had only just shaken off the dreadful black water of the canal under the ice and now here was more dark water, rising up in her imagination.

"It's called 'Flood'," said Jason as he began to read.

CHAPTER 4

It had been raining for days and days. The four friends thought it would never end. Every day when they came to school they got soaked – and then soaked again on the way home. There was already talk on the news about flooding.

There was a small river running through the town, but no one could ever remember it flooding. The canals helped to control the flow of water. But this year was different.

After school, Maya stood on the banks of the river with Carla, Jason and Tomas, watching as the water level rose and rose. The river gleamed in the lights from the shops and houses as it swirled past. The water looked black, like oil.

It was exciting and scary at the same time. The police were keeping everyone clear of the danger, but Maya and Carla and Jason and Tomas kept moving along, peering past the gaps in the onlookers and emergency services.

They decided to go further to get to a less busy bit of the riverside so they could get a better view. They went under the underpass and reached a clear patch on the riverside path which hadn't been cordoned off yet.

Maya squeezed past a girl in a silver hooded coat and the others followed. They reached the edge of the riverbank and gasped at how high the river was now and how fast it was moving. It was halfway up the wall on the opposite side – the wall that ran alongside the common between St Matthew's Church and the factory.

Little bits of the wall were breaking off and falling into the water. The friends could see the wall trembling with the force of the river. Then, all of a sudden, it collapsed and tumbled into the water. Lumps of stone and earth splashed down.

"Wow!" said Jason. "Maybe we should head back."

Maya was just turning away when she saw something slip out of the earth on the opposite side of the river and slide into the water like a seal. But what could be coming out of the earth like that?

Then there was another one. Then another.

They slid out and under the water so fast, she couldn't get a proper view of what they were. The river just took them and carried them away like they had never even been there.

Then Maya was sure she saw bodies shoot past under the dark water.

"Look!" Maya said, pulling Carla towards her and pointing.

"What?" said Carla.

"There!" shouted Maya.

"What was that?" said Jason, coming over. "Did you see it?"

"Yeah," said Tomas. "But what was it?"

"I don't know," said Carla. "But I didn't like it. It's made my knees go wobbly. Can we go now?"

"I know it sounds mad, but they looked like bodies falling into the river," said Maya. "Frozen bodies."

"How can they be bodies, Maya?" said Jason.

"Wait," said Tomas. "My dad told me the common used to be a burial ground. Back in medieval times."

"But even if that's true," said Jason. "Any bodies in there must be centuries old. They'd just be bones by now, wouldn't they? Why would they be frozen? It's not even that cold."

"Maybe we should tell someone anyway," said Carla.

"Tell who?" said Tomas.

"The police," said Carla. "There are loads of them here."

"And say what?" said Tomas. "I don't even know what I saw. It was probably just a trick of the light or something."

"A trick of the light?" said Maya. "What does that even mean?"

But all the same, Maya was not about to wander up to a police officer and say she'd seen stiff, frozen bodies falling into the river. The strange thing was that she had been sure of what she had seen at the time, but now it felt impossible.

*

Maya did not sleep much that night. She kept seeing the bodies slipping into the inky waters over and over again. She woke up to a message from Carla about the floods with a link to a news report about the rising waters. The shops and houses along Canal Street were already flooded.

It was exciting for a while to have her town on the news, but it wasn't exciting for the roads to be filling up with water.

The waters kept rising and rising, over the common and heading for the sports field. But the school was safe. It was right at the top of a hill. Even so, school had been cancelled because many of the students couldn't get there – and because many of their homes had been flooded.

Maya's estate was nowhere near the flooding, but she had a good view of the water from their flat. She could see streets filled with black water, reflecting street lights and signs. It made Maya think of those things in the water by the common – but she had become less and less certain of what she had seen.

Then, strangely, the floodwaters retreated just as suddenly as they had risen and the clear-up began. The news crews left and the town started to count the cost of the flooding. The school was reopened.

Maya was secretly pleased that they were going back to school. The problems caused by the flood had been interesting for a while just because it was something new, but it had fast become really irritating.

She was happy to have her normal life back – hanging out with Carla, Jason and Tomas on the walkway by the lockers at school. At the end of their first day back they looked through the window at the town and talked about people they knew whose homes had been flooded. From the school window there was no sign that there had even been a flood. At least not at first ...

As the four friends watched, it started to rain. It rained so hard that they could not even see the other side of the playground. It hammered against the windows and thundered on the roof. They could just make out through the fog of rain that water had started to rise up. It was surging towards the school from the common, moving fast. They weren't the only people to see it. There were yells and shouts from all over the school.

"How's that even possible?" said Jason. "The school's on a hill. How is that water heading this way?"

But however it was happening, the water was steadily rising and was soon surrounding the whole school. Still the rain came down. It did not seem possible there could be that much water in the clouds.

"We're going to get stuck here! Come on!" shouted Maya. She pushed Carla towards the door and turned to see if the boys were following.

"You're not going anywhere," said Miss Miller from behind them. "It's dangerous out there. We don't know how much water we're due. The best thing we can do is stay here on the upper floor until the emergency services arrive. They'll tell us what to do next. Is that understood? No one is to leave this building."

There was lots of muttering at the idea of this and a bit of panic too. The crowd of children pushed forwards and back, not sure of where to go.

"Stop pushing!" shouted Miss Miller. "You can text your parents and carers and tell them what's happening."

"There's no signal, Miss," said Maya.

"No signal?" said Miss Miller. "Oh, for goodness' sake."

Miss Miller looked at her phone, but her face quickly fell. All the children around her held up their phones too, to show they also had no signal.

"It must be the flood," said Miss Miller. "I'm sure it will get sorted out soon. Don't panic."

Miss Miller was trying to sound relaxed, but Maya could hear more than a touch of panic in her voice.

Her plea didn't make a difference anyway as the children pushed and shoved. They stumbled down the stairs as the water washed across the car park and playground and slapped up against the doors.

"Calm down!" shouted Miss Miller.

But there was no calming anyone now. The lights were flickering and going out one by one. It was only the afternoon, yet it was as dark as night. Maya could hear some sobbing behind her. She did not feel far from tears herself.

"What are we going to do?" said Jason.

"What can we do?" said Carla with a shrug.

Maya groaned, feeling frustrated.

"It's like Miss says," said Tomas. "We just need to wait for help."

But suddenly everything changed. It was still raining, but the water level had dropped dramatically. The flood seemed to be retreating back down the hill. Within minutes the playground was almost clear. There were just a few rubbish bags and piles of rags the water had left behind.

There was a huge cheer from all the children as the lights went back on, and even Miss Miller joined in.

"Well, that's a relief," she said.

"Can we go now, Miss?" said Maya. "The water's mostly gone."

"I think we should just wait and see what's happening first," said Miss Miller.

Then Maya was sure she saw one of the bags of rubbish move.

"Jason," she said. "Did you see that?"

He had. So had Tomas.

By the time they got Carla's attention, everyone had seen.

The bags of rubbish were not rags or rubbish at all. They were people and they were getting up.

Everyone inside screamed, including Miss Miller, as the figures in the playground began to walk slowly towards the building.

They were dressed in strange clothes –
hooded cloaks and ragged shawls. They looked
like the people in old fairy stories, except it
would have to be the scariest fairy story ever
because these people had grim faces and were
shuffling, their eyes wide open like they were in
a trance.

There was more screaming from the pupils,
but the only way out was past the zombies and
no one was going to do that. Everyone turned
to Miss Miller, who looked like she was about to
faint. She was just staring and staring as the
shuffling figures got closer and closer to the
school. The only person not jumping up and
down and yelling was a girl in a silver hooded
coat who stood with her back to Maya in the
corridor.

The lights above the playground and car
park suddenly went off again, causing yet more
screaming. The shuffling figures could only now

be seen by the light from inside the school and only then because they were so close.

Then the indoor lights started to flicker. Before anyone could move or scream, the figures burst into the building and all the lights went out.

"Miss Miller!" yelled Maya.

*

Her shout seemed to jolt Maya out of the story and back into the library.

"Maya, for goodness' sake," said Mrs Varga. "What is wrong with you today? What must Mr Kumar make of us?"

"Are you all right, Maya?" asked Mr Kumar. "Would you like to go and see the nurse?"

"I ... I ... I ... I was there," said Maya. "In the flood and the school and the zombies."

"It was a very gripping story," Mr Kumar said. "I felt like I was there myself."

"No," said Maya. "I really was there. I mean, really."

"I see," said Mr Kumar, casting a glance towards Mrs Varga. She rolled her eyes.

"Anyway," said Mr Kumar. "That was very good, Jason. Well done. Anyone else?"

Maya put her hand up – to her own surprise as much as everyone else's. Mrs Varga opened her mouth to speak, but Mr Kumar got in first.

"You've got a story, Maya?" he said.

"Yes," said Maya.

"Well, that's great," said Mr Kumar. "Will you share it with the class?"

Maya nodded. She actually wanted to. She felt like she needed to. It suddenly felt like the story was scuttling around in the back of her head and she needed to let it out. It was all so clear in her mind that all she really had to do was describe what she was seeing.

"My idea is about Jack Frost, sir," said Maya. "You know – thinking of him as a person."

"Yes," said Mr Kumar. "Excellent. I've always thought Jack Frost was a bit of a creepy idea. Someone – or something – that creeps about spreading frost while we're all asleep."

"I remember my mum saying that Jack Frost had been in the night when I was a kid," Maya said. "I really thought that there was someone called Jack Frost who brought the cold with him. I suppose it stuck in my mind."

But as she said this, Maya realised she hadn't thought about Jack Frost for years.

"Well, then," said Mr Kumar. "If it has stuck in your mind all this time, there's probably a great story there. Let's hear it."

CHAPTER 5

Maya hated the school Winterfest. It was so
boring – a fundraising event with stalls selling
all kinds of stuff, none of which anyone could
possibly want. The only good thing was the food
stalls, especially the baking stall. Bella Willis
was really annoying, but her mother was an
amazing baker and always brought a whole load
of cakes.

Maya did not understand why Carla had
been so keen to come to Winterfest. It was a
Saturday and there was something so wrong
about being at school during the weekend!

Maya would have talked Carla out of it, too, if it hadn't been for Jason and Tomas agreeing with Carla. Now here the four friends were and the stalls were probably even more boring than usual.

Maya's three friends soon wandered off. Maya was just about to spin round and head outside when she saw a stall that was very different to the others.

It looked more like something from a vintage market or even a stall from hundreds of years ago. It was wooden with coloured flags hanging over it and it was filled with all kinds of things. But the thing that caught Maya's eye was the puppet.

It was wooden and was clearly very old, despite still being in its original packaging with JACK FROST written on the cardboard box. It looked as if it had been in someone's attic for a long time. Maya wanted to ask if she could have a look, but there was no one there to ask. So she carefully took the puppet out of the box.

The puppet was dressed in pale blue and white, its clothes covered in sparkling silver sequins and tiny pearl-like beads. There were strings coming from his jointed arms, legs and head, but they were cut and frayed and weren't attached to anything.

The Jack Frost puppet's face was long and thin with a sharp nose and chin. He wore a pointed hat that curled back and ended in a silver bell. His legs and arms were bent like he was doing a strange little dance or was creeping along.

His shoes were long and pointed too. But not as long and pointed as his fingers, which were curled in front of his face, ending in long and sharp fingernails. So sharp in fact that one of the nails jabbed Maya painfully in the arm.

"Ow!" said Maya, dropping the puppet.
There was a tiny drop of blood where the
puppet's pointed fingernail had pricked her arm.

She was about to go in search of the
others when she saw a sign on the stall saying
"Everything Free". *How does that work?*
Maya thought. Winterfest was meant to be a
fundraising thing. That puppet must be worth
something – collectors might pay a lot of money
for it.

Maya looked around. The sign said
"Everything Free", so taking it wouldn't be
stealing, would it? She picked up the puppet and
went to find Carla and the others.

"You didn't buy that, did you?" said Carla as
Maya came over. "With actual money?"

"No," said Maya. "It was free! Can you
believe it?"

"Er … yes," said Jason, raising an eyebrow.

"Everything on the stall was free," Maya said.

"What stall?" asked Carla.

Maya turned to point at it, but she couldn't see the stall anywhere.

"That's weird," Maya said. "The people running it must have gone."

"Shame," said Tomas. "Did they have loads of stuff like this?"

"Shut up," said Maya. "It was a really cool stall. It had tons of really old things on it. I think this might be worth something."

"Yeah," said Carla. "About five pence."

"It is so creepy," said Tomas.

"No it isn't," said Maya. "Don't be horrible."

"But it really is," said Jason. "So creepy."

"You're just jealous," said Maya.

"Of what?" said Carla. "Why would we be jealous?"

"Because I've got a vintage doll and you haven't."

Carla rolled her eyes. "Yeah?" she said. "I don't think so. Who wants a creepy puppet anyway?"

Jason asked to have a look and Maya handed the puppet over.

"There's a label," said Jason. "See? Here on the back. It says 'Jack Frost – KEEP WARM'."

"That's a bit of a weird thing to say about a Jack Frost puppet, huh?" said Tomas. "Isn't his whole thing about being cold?"

"Maybe it's not talking about the puppet," said Jason. "Maybe it means that *you* need to

keep warm because of the frost. You know –
Jack Frost."

"That's really clever, Jason," said Maya.

"Or maybe ..." said Carla. "Maybe it's saying
you have to keep the puppet warm. You know –
never let it get cold."

"Why?" said Maya.

"Well, I don't know, do I?" said Carla. "It's not
my stupid puppet."

Maya rolled her eyes. She put the puppet
down on the table.

"I'm just going to the loo," she said. "Keep
an eye on Jack Frost for me."

When she came out again, the hall was
full of parents and children milling about. She
made her way over to her friends at the table,
but the puppet was gone.

"What have you done with it?" asked Maya.

"Done with what?" said Carla.

"You know what," said Maya. "Jack Frost."

"The manky puppet?" said Carla. "Why would I do anything with that?"

"I know you took it," said Maya. "Give it back."

"Carla's been with us the whole time, Maya," said Jason.

"Oh, you're always sticking up for her," said Maya.

"No I'm not," said Jason. "It's just true. She's been here with us. She hasn't taken your puppet, Maya."

"Well, someone has, so who was it?" Maya demanded.

She gave them all her sternest look, but none of them cracked. They were all telling the truth. It must have been someone else. But who?

Maya spotted Miss Miller and told her about the missing puppet.

"Well, the Winterfest will be packing up soon, Maya. I'll leave a note in reception and maybe someone will hand it in. A puppet you say?"

"Make sure you write 'creepy puppet'," said Carla.

Miss Miller chuckled as she headed off.

"Someone's stolen it," said Maya. "Come on, let's see if we can spot the thief as they leave."

So they wandered round the hall trying to spot any suspicious items being carried outside.

But there was nothing. Most of the stalls had already packed up.

"We've got to go, Maya," said Carla. "Everyone's leaving."

"I'm not going before I find that puppet," said Maya.

"Do any of you know anything about this?" said a voice behind them.

They all turned to see one of the school dinner ladies holding the Jack Frost puppet by its long arm.

"Yay!" said Maya. "I knew it would turn up!"

"No you didn't," said Tomas. "You thought it had been stolen."

"Whatever," said Maya. "At least it's here now."

"I suppose you think that's funny!" said the dinner lady, Mrs Pimm. "Frightened the bloomin' life out of me, it did. I might have known you four would be involved."

"Hey," said Carla. "That's not fair. We haven't done anything."

"Then how did this thing get in the freezer?" Mrs Pimm asked.

"The freezer?" said Maya.

She could see now that Jack Frost was glistening and sparkling, covered with icy frost.

"It's not hygienic," said Mrs Pimm. "We'll get in trouble with the council. Who knows where this thing has been? What is it anyway? Horrible, creepy thing."

"See?" said Carla to Maya. "Creepy."

"Oh, shut up," said Maya. "Thanks, Mrs Pimm. Sorry about that."

Mrs Pimm seemed relieved to hand the puppet over.

"And whose is this coat?" said Mrs Pimm, holding up a silver coat with a fur-lined hood.

"Never seen it before, Miss," said Maya – but as soon as she said that, she was not sure it was true.

"I'll leave it in reception," said Mrs Pimm. "You should be getting off now anyway. You're the last ones."

Maya had to put the puppet down on a table again. It was too cold to hold. It stung her fingers.

"So you see – none of us took your stupid puppet," said Carla to Maya. "I think you should say sorry."

"But how did he get into the freezer?" Maya said. "It's not like he'd do it on his own."

"Can we just go now?" said Carla. "I'm starving."

"Wait," said Jason. "Where's it gone?"

"Where's what gone?" said Tomas.

"The puppet!" Jason said. "The Jack Frost puppet! It was right there and now it's not."

But then Maya saw something moving out of the corner of her eye at the end of the room. She wasn't sure what it was, but it made her feel funny. There was something about the way it moved. Fast and then stop, fast and then stop. She had to force herself to look, and she felt like she was dropping down a lift shaft as she realised the moving thing was Jack Frost, the puppet.

It was scampering and skidding along, waving its arms about this way and that. Wherever the puppet went, it left a trail of sparkles, throwing them from the end of its sharp fingernails. Soon that end of the room was shining with frost and the frost started to climb up the windows in big beautiful patterns.

"What the hell?" said Carla as the Jack Frost puppet skidded out from under a table.

"How is that thing moving?" said Jason.

"I don't know," said Maya. "But I don't think we should hang around to find out."

"Keep warm!" said Carla. "See? The puppet wasn't supposed to get cold. Now it has."

"What are you on about, Carla?" said Maya.

"The cold must have brought the puppet to life!" said Carla.

At that moment the Jack Frost puppet leapt up onto the Christmas tree and pulled it over, smashing the fairy lights.

"Whoah!" said Tomas.

There was a crackling, spitting noise and then sparks showered out from the tree, starting a fire among the fake presents underneath.

The four friends didn't move at first. It was Jason who was first to react, shouting "Fire!" at the top of his voice.

The sprinklers came on, and everything – including them – got soaked. Carla started to laugh.

But not for long. The puppet scuttled towards the four friends like a monkey, its long fingernails scritch-scratching on the floor. Everything Jack Frost touched turned to shimmering ice. He danced around the room, freezing everything. Even the water from the sprinklers was frozen into a cascade of sparkling icicles.

Now Jack Frost crept slowly towards them. The grin on his face seemed even wider than before, his teeth gleaming like tiny icicles. The puppet was covered in frost too now – tiny white spikes of ice.

The four friends found they were frozen to the spot as Jack Frost came closer and closer. Maya felt the puppet creeping up her clothes, until his fingernails were at her neck and face. She opened her mouth to scream, but frost filled her mouth and froze her tongue into silence.

*

Suddenly Maya was back in the safety of the library. But her heart was still galloping. She was gasping. She couldn't speak. She had terrified herself with her own story.

"Are you OK?" said Mr Kumar.

"What?" said Maya. "What? Me? Yeah. I'm fine."

But she wasn't fine. She felt like she was losing her mind. How could a story seem so real? What was going on? Next to Maya, Winter smiled to herself and kept writing.

There was something about the way Winter smiled that Maya did not like. It was as if she was enjoying a private joke.

"Wait a minute," said Maya. "It was you!"

"Me?" said Winter.

"Yeah," Maya said. "It was your coat. It was you who put the puppet in the freezer!"

"I put the puppet in the freezer?" said the Winter. "In your story?"

Maya realised how stupid that sounded. All the same, Maya had the sense that Winter had been in each one of the stories somehow.

"Well, that was another great story, I'm sure we all agree," said Mr Kumar. He looked at his watch. "Well, that seems to be it for today. We've run out of time, sadly. Well done, everyone. Hopefully those of you who didn't get a chance to read your story today will get another chance later on, if you'd like. I'm sure Miss Miller will be keen to hear them."

Winter just ignored Mr Kumar and stood up, holding her sheets of paper.

"My story is about what was here before the school was built," Winter said.

What is going on? thought Maya. *How come Winter gets to just do whatever she likes?*

"Sir," said Maya. "You said the story had to be set in the present. She's doing something set in the past."

Winter just smiled at Maya and began her story.

"There was a village here. A long time ago. In the days of wood and horses. Back before any of you or any of this."

Maya scowled. Who cared? She didn't want any more stories. She just wanted to go home. But just as with the other stories, Maya felt like she was there, living it, not just hearing it as Winter began her tale.

CHAPTER 6

The village was only small, just a scattering of houses and farms. But it was a happy place. The villagers were used to hard winters. Winter was just part of life. Winter could be beautiful.

It was a time to gather round the fire. Parents told stories about Jack Frost and children made snowmen. The marshes that had flooded in the autumn froze over and children dared each other to go further and further out on the ice.

But this winter was different. It was harder than anyone could remember and seemed like it would go on for ever. The villagers thought it was the end of the world. For some of them, it was.

The sky was dark all day and it was bitterly cold. The crops were frozen into the ground and ruined. The earth was as hard as iron. Humans and animals huddled together in the barns for warmth. Many died from the cold.

The ground was too hard to bury the dead, so the bodies were stored above the ground, where the cold preserved them. Like they were in a freezer, Winter joked.

That's not something to laugh about, thought Maya, totally engrossed in the world of the story. She saw the huddle of small wooden houses, their thatched roofs heavy with snow, icicles hanging down. Surrounding them were frozen marshes that stretched off into the mist on the horizon.

The people of the village wondered if they would ever see the sun again. Were they being punished? They looked around for someone to blame.

There had always been whispers about the miller's daughter. People said she was a witch.

Now the villagers said that she must have cursed the weather and it was her fault that the winter was just going on and on.

They had no evidence or proof. How could they? But they were ignorant and superstitious. The villagers' accusations were mostly based on the way she looked – so strange and pale and other-worldly.

The elders of the village gathered together and there was a kind of trial for the girl. But it wasn't real justice, of course.

The girl defended herself. She said it was nothing to do with her. She was innocent. But they wouldn't believe her. Even her own family turned against her.

The more she denied any responsibility for the terrible weather, the more the villagers became obsessed with the idea that she had cursed them. The girl begged them to believe her, but they would not listen.

After no time at all, the old men talked amongst themselves and decided she was guilty.

The girl was dragged away and locked in a barn. She was terrified.

The villagers threatened her, shouting at her from outside. The children yelled at her, calling her a witch and running away, laughing.

The elders decided the girl must be punished if the village was to survive.

She was led through the village. The people crowded round her. They pointed at her and shouted, "Winter!" All of their hatred for the weather was directed at this girl.

They sent her out of the village. She was forced to walk out across the frozen water of the marshes, to die alone in the dark while the villagers went back to their fires. They thought killing her meant they could kill winter.

"I curse all who live here for all time!" the girl yelled from the marshes. "Just like winter, I will always return!"

In the morning the villagers found the girl frozen to death. Her pale blue eyes were open. Her skin was almost as blue as her eyes and covered in frost.

The curse the girl had yelled before she died seeped into the ground and into the trees and into the houses that were built on the drained marshes. It even entered the walls of the school that was built on the very site of the village, centuries later. One day, the girl would return ...

*

"So she really was a witch then?" said Maya.

"No," said Winter with a smile. "The curse was powered by the collected evil of the cruel villagers. The girl was just a mirror, reflecting back their own cold hatred."

"Yeah, but she must have been a witch to do that or—" Maya started to say.

"I wasn't a witch!" yelled Winter.

Maya stared at her. She had never seen such a dramatic change in anyone. Winter had been as still as a statue before her outburst. Now her face was blazing with an icy fury.

"So then the action of the story moves to the present day," Winter went on as if nothing had happened. "To this very day. A supply teacher comes to the school and does a lesson about writing creepy stories set in wintertime. There isn't just this new teacher at the school – there's a new girl too. Her name is Winter.

"Winter's skin is almost as white as snow. Mr Kumar asks everyone to come up with creepy stories on the theme of winter and the new girl begins to write and write as Maya watches from across the table.

"The teacher asks if anyone wants to read their story out loud and four students do. One story is about snow, the next about ice, followed by a story about a flood and one about frost. Then Winter tells a story about a girl who was brutally killed by the ignorant villagers that lived where this school now stands.

"Maya assumes the story Winter tells must be made up. Must be a story. Must be from her imagination.

"But it isn't a story. It isn't made up. That girl really existed. Those murdering villagers existed too. They really did leave the girl to die in the cold and dark. Her family really did stand by and yell just like everyone else. No one tried to help her. They really did call her Winter. They really did think that by killing her they could kill winter. But you can't kill winter. Winter always returns."

Maya stared at Winter. There was such an intense look on her face. It was like she hated everyone and everything around her. Maya had never seen an expression like it and it made her shiver.

It was getting colder in the library too. Everyone's breath was rising up like smoke and Maya wondered why no one else seemed to have noticed.

No one was moving. Winter seemed to be the only person who could speak. She carried on reading her story as everyone else in the library just stared ahead, their breath rising up in thin white clouds.

"Winter continues with her story while the teacher and the students just sit in silence," Winter went on. "They have no idea that Winter is even here. Only Maya can see her."

Maya wondered why Mr Kumar was just letting Winter go on, but he seemed to be in a kind of trance. He looked like a shop dummy, just staring in Winter's direction. So was everyone else, including Carla, Jason and Tomas.

It was getting darker and darker outside. Maya looked out at the sports field and the sky was almost black. Where it wasn't black it was a weird colour – grey-white, like old bones.

Maya could feel her jaw clenching shut with the cold. Her teeth were clamped so tightly together she thought they might shatter and go clattering across the table like tiny ice cubes.

She was rigid and could only move her eyes. She could see that Carla and Tomas and Jason at the next table were the same. Everyone was the same. All except Winter, who carried on reading like everything was fine.

Maya wanted to call out, but she couldn't. Her vocal cords were frozen, along with the rest of her body. Maya wanted to yell out that this new girl was the same girl from Winter's story. She was the girl the villagers had called Winter to punish her. She was the same girl who had frozen to death on the marshes. The same girl who had cursed the village.

"The new girl carries on reading," continued Winter, "and while she reads, the room becomes colder and colder. No one notices that any of this is happening. They are all just as stupid as the villagers were. They thought they could destroy Winter. Everyone in the library is slowly freezing to death, just like poor Winter had frozen to death."

Maya watched Winter's breath rise up in wisps too as she read her story, but she didn't shiver or shake. Her hands weren't screwed into fists. Winter looked more relaxed now than she had at the start. There was even a smile on her pale face, but it wasn't a pleasant one.

It was so clear to Maya now that the new girl wasn't just untouched by all this – she was causing it. It was all her. The words that Winter read out were coming true. If she wasn't stopped, they would all come true – every last one of them. They would all die. Maya had to do something.

Maya used her last remaining spark of life and strength to lunge forward and grab the sheets of paper out of Winter's hands and rip them up.

*

The instant Maya tore the pages, the room returned to normal, the deathly coldness gone.

"Who's stupid now?!" yelled Maya, getting to her feet and pointing at Winter.

"Maya!" shouted Mrs Varga. "What on earth are you doing?"

"What?" said Maya. "I had to. Didn't you see what was happening? Didn't you see what she was doing?"

"Who?" said Mr Kumar.

"Her!" said Maya, pointing to Winter.

But Winter wasn't there any more. Nor was her bag or any of her stuff.

"What?" said Maya. "Where'd she go?"

The rest of the class started to laugh. Maya slumped back, her head down, embarrassed and confused. Everything was normal. Everything was just like it was before Winter had walked into the library. Carla was giggling, like she always did.

"I saved your lives!" shouted Maya.

There was a lot of laughter at that.

"Maya, chill," whispered Jason.

Now it was Maya's turn to laugh.

"Chill?" she said, and laughed again. "Chill? Is that a joke?"

"OK, everyone," said Mr Kumar. "Please hang on to your stories and make sure your name is on them. You'll be continuing them with Miss Miller next week."

There was a scraping of chairs and rustling of paper as everyone filled their bags and hoisted them onto their backs. Maya quickly gathered up the pieces of Winter's story and rammed them into her bag.

Maya was distracted by looking for Winter as she and her friends headed off to their next class. It was in the music block on the other side of the playground. Maya searched every group they passed for any sign of Winter but did not see her anywhere.

"You all right?" said Tomas. "You were acting pretty odd in there."

"Yeah, well," said Maya. "Not as odd as her."

"As odd as who?" said Tomas.

"As odd as her!" Maya said. "The new girl! Winter!"

"What are you even talking about?" said Carla. "What new girl?"

"What?" said Maya. "The one in the lesson just now."

"There was no new girl in the lesson," said Carla. "I think you're losing it."

Maya looked at Carla, but this wasn't a wind-up. Carla really didn't know who Maya was talking about. How was that possible?

"Come on," Maya said. "She was tall. Skinny. Jet-black hair. Super pale. Like she'd never been out in the sun. Like, ever."

"Yeah?" said Carla with a smile. "Super-pale girl. OK ..."

"You must have seen her," said Maya. "She was sitting at my table. Silver coat with a fur-trimmed hood."

Carla scowled at her.

"You were on your own, Maya," said Carla. "You OK?"

"Are *you* OK?" shouted Maya. "She was right there! She read a story out. She told us all about the village that used to be here before the school. She said how the villagers killed a girl because they blamed her for the cold weather."

"Maya," said Carla. "Seriously. This isn't funny, you know. No one read a whole story out. That never happened. A few people read out the start of their stories – that was all."

Maya stared at Carla – then at Jason and Tomas. They had to be winding her up. But Carla wasn't that sharp. She wouldn't have been able to keep up the pretence. Carla would be laughing by now if this was a joke.

"You read a story about skating, Carla," said Maya, close to tears now. "And you read one about snowmen, Tomas. And you about a flood, Jason."

Jason, Tomas and Carla looked at each other and then back at Maya.

"Were they any good then, these stories?" said Carla.

"They were really scary. They felt so real. It was like I was living them."

"Wow," said Jason. "I wish I really had written something that good."

"But you did," said Maya. "You all did. I don't understand. I was always getting us into trouble in them."

"That sounds right," said Carla with a grin.

"But you saved us in the end?" said Tomas.

"Yeah," said Maya. "I did. I saved everyone."

"Well, then," said Carla, giving her a hug. "Thanks."

"Maybe you fell asleep in the lesson, Maya," Jason said. "You were saying how tired you were. You might have heard bits of the stories in your sleep and dreamed the rest."

Frustrated, Maya was about to yell at Jason, but actually she found the idea of having fallen asleep more appealing. Maybe that did explain things.

"Wait!" shouted Maya, stopping in the middle of the playground and searching in her bag. "I've got her story!"

"Whose story?" said Carla.

"Winter's story. The girl you say wasn't there," said Maya. "That's how I stopped the magic. I grabbed her story and ripped it up! If Winter wasn't there, then who wrote this?"

Maya pulled out the sheets of paper and slapped them down on top of her bag, flattening them out. Her friends leaned in to see.

Maya pointed at it. "See! I told you."

"I thought you said you ripped them up," said Jason.

"I did," said Maya.

She looked back at the pages. To her amazement, they were whole. They were a bit creased, but they had clearly never been torn.

"Anyway, this is *your* writing," said Carla, pointing to the top sheet.

"It can't be," said Maya.

"Yeah," said Jason. "It's got one of those doodles you always—"

"What?" said Maya, grabbing it. "I didn't write that! She wrote it. I don't understand."

"I think you're coming down with something," said Carla. "Seriously. What does it say anyway?"

Carla lifted the page to her face and started to read very slowly. "OK – it's called 'Winter'. Although that's where your name is supposed to be, Maya."

Carla started to read …

"Maya woke with a jolt when the music started playing, not sure for a moment where she was. She gave her radio alarm clock a smack to stop the music, knocking it off the bedside table and sending it clattering to the floor …"

As Carla read a few more words, clouds started to spread across the sky. It became so dark she had to peer at the page to continue. Carla's breath rose up as a little cloud from her mouth.

"Woah!" said Tomas. "It's freezing!"

Snowflakes started to fall. One or two at first but very soon a flurry and then came a thick downpour of fat white snowflakes as Carla continued to read.

"Stop!" shouted Maya.

"Rude," said Carla, carrying on.

"No!" shouted Maya. She grabbed the paper from Carla's hands, ripping it to shreds. She threw the pieces away and they drifted off on the breeze like snowflakes.

"What has got into you?" said Carla.

"Oh man, I love it when it snows," said Jason.

"Me too," said Tomas. "Maybe school will have to close early."

"That wasn't even Winter's story," said Maya. "That's just about me. That's what happened this morning before I came into school. Remember – I told you I'd had a nightmare."

"Well, you wrote it, Maya," said Carla. "I don't know why you're being so weird about it."

"But I *didn't* write it," said Maya. "I swear. Wait. There she is!"

"Who?" Carla said.

"The new girl. Winter. The one who's doing all this."

Winter was heading out of the school gates, wearing a silver padded coat with a white fur hood. She stopped as she heard Maya's voice and turned to face the four friends.

"Do you see her?" shouted Maya, grabbing hold of Carla.

"All right, all right," said Carla. "We see her. But this is the first time I've laid eyes on her, Maya."

"You have to believe me," said Maya. "I don't know what's going on, but she's not just some random new girl at the school. She's ..."

But Maya did not know how to explain what Winter was.

"Come on," said Maya. "Let's follow her!"

The others trailed after Maya reluctantly, muttering about getting into trouble for leaving the school grounds. But she took no notice.

Winter walked straight on towards the common between the river and the canal. Ahead, the chimney of the old factory rose above the bare trees at the common's edge.

The four friends ran to catch up with Winter just as she reached the edge of the trees. The snow was still falling heavily out of the yellowy grey sky.

"Oi!" shouted Maya.

Winter slowly turned round as they caught her up. Her blue grey eyes shimmered like frozen pools.

"What the ...?" said Jason. "Look at her face."

Maya and the others looked. Winter's face was almost blue and her skin was covered in tiny spikes of frost, like fur.

She's got that evil smile again, thought Maya with a shiver.

"Feeling cold?" said Winter.

The temperature had plummeted. The sky had darkened again and the snow turned to rain, falling heavily. They were all soaked in moments.

Then, just as suddenly, the rain stopped and snow began to fall again. Big fat snowflakes at first, drifting down like feathers, but they soon became small, swirled around by the wind. The snow was so thick and hard it covered the four friends and froze them to the spot.

"Ha," said Winter. "You look like snowmen. Four ugly snowmen. You see? Winter always returns."

Winter's smile grew and she moved towards the four friends, parting the swirling snow as she walked.

"Th ... This is my nightmare," said Maya.

"Mine too," said Carla and Tomas and Jason together. They all realised at the same time. But it was too late. They were freezing. They could not move. They tried to call out, but the air in their lungs seemed to freeze.

*

Maya woke with a jolt when the music started playing, not sure for a moment where she was. She gave her radio alarm clock a smack to stop the music, knocking it off the bedside table and sending it clattering to the floor.

Maya jumped up to check if the alarm clock was broken. Her mum had bought it for her to make sure she always woke up for school. She was relieved to see it still seemed to be working.

Maya opened the curtains, squinting into the cloudy daylight. She looked out over the estate, across the canal, past the old factory and the common towards the school. She suddenly had an intense feeling that something bad was going to happen.

She just didn't know what ...

ANOTHER HAUNTING TALE FROM CHRIS PRIESTLEY

seven ghosts

CHRIS PRIESTLEY

ISBN: 978-1-78112-894-7

Our books are tested
for children and young people by
children and young people.

Thanks to everyone who consulted on
a manuscript for their time and effort in
helping us to make our books better
for our readers.